For Rosemary
with all my best
Beni Montresor
1983

P9-ELT-243

Beni Montresor
The Witches of Venice

DOUBLEDAY

NEW YORK   LONDON   TORONTO   SYDNEY   AUCKLAND

Published by Doubleday, a division of Bantam Doubleday Dell Publishing Group, Inc. 666 Fifth Avenue, New York, New York 10103   **Doubleday** and the portrayal of an anchor with a dolphin are trademarks of Doubleday, a division of Bantam Doubleday Dell Publishing Group, Inc.   Library of Congress Cataloging-in-Publication Data   Montresor, Beni. The witches of Venice / by Beni Montresor. p.   cm.   Summary: Rejected by the King and Queen of Venice, a lonely flower-plant boy seeks a flower-plant girl imprisoned by the Witches of the Grand Canal.   [1. Venice (Italy)—Fiction.   2. Witches—Fiction.   3. Fairy tales.]   I. Title. PZ8.M769Wi   1989   [E]—dc19   88-27158 CIP AC   ISBN-0-385-26354-6 (Trade) ISBN 0-385-26355-4 (Library)   R.L: 3.1   Copyright © 1989 by Beni Montresor   All Rights Reserved   Printed in Italy   1089

*I*n the ancient city of Venice there once lived a King of great power and a Queen covered with jewels from head to foot. But they had no son to inherit their throne, so they fretted and could not sleep well at all.

The situation was intolerable. The King thought and thought, and finally he summoned all the philosophers of the world. But after days and days of discussions, the philosophers said, "We are sorry, Your Majesty. We have no solution."

Then one day two Fairies of the Lagoon came to the King. Holding out a leafy plant, they sang:

"Plant this in your garden
And when it blooms at dawn
You will find to your surprise
A little child is born."

"You stupid girls! Children aren't born from plants!" roared the King, and he threw the plant out of the window.

The next morning the kitchen maid was sweeping the courtyard. When she saw the plant, half dried and almost dead, she said, "A plant is to be planted," and planted it in the middle of the garden.

After a while the Sun came out and warmed the poor plant. Suddenly it blossomed. The Sun, beaming with joy, said, "How are you, my little one?"

Out of the plant hopped a little boy, merry and rosy-cheeked, and the little boy replied, "Much better, thank you."

The kitchen maid, who was at the window, saw everything. She ran to the throne room and exclaimed, "Your Majesty, a little boy has come out of the plant!"

"Liar!" roared the King. But then he added, "Let us go and see."

They went to the garden, and when they were in front of the little boy, the kitchen maid said, "You see? It is a boy."

"It is a plant!" screamed the King.

"You are the King, so you must be right!" The kitchen maid exclaimed with admiration.

The King solemnly decreed: "Because this plant is a plant it must remain planted in the garden." He called for twelve guards and put them all around the garden wall so the little boy could not escape.

The Sun came in every day and made the juiciest fruits in the world grow for the little boy. The Wind came too, and to amuse him, sent leaves spinning into the air.

But it was useless, for the child was so sad that no one could make him smile.

Then one day the Wind rushed to the little boy and whispered, "Hide! Witches are coming!"

"We've come to see the little flower-plant boy," said two Witches of the Grand Canal, flying into the garden. They searched above and below every leaf, but all in vain.

"You forgot to look into the watering can," called the kitchen maid from the window.

"Oh!" they exclaimed when they pulled the child out of the watering can. "He has sad eyes, just like our little flower-plant girl. How tiresome!" They looked up to the kitchen maid and said, "Tell the King and Queen they are invited to our Great Summer Ball."

"What little flower-plant girl?" the boy called, but the Witches had already flown away.

From that day on the little flower-plant boy thought of nothing but the little flower-plant girl. But how could he escape and find her?

One morning he gathered all the dry branches he could find and built a huge pigeon with two wheels attached to its feet.

"Get ready," he said to the Wind, "I am going to find the little flower-plant girl and play wonderful games with her."

"What about the King?" whispered the Wind.

"The King doesn't like flower-plant children," answered the little boy. Climbing inside the pigeon, he whispered, "Blow!" And so the Wind did, but at the gate there stood the King's guards keeping watch.

"Blow, blow faster!" whispered the little boy.

The Wind whirled around and around until the guards' eyes were blinded by dust. Then the pigeon slipped safely through the garden gate!

Huffing and puffing, the Wind moved the pigeon across the entire city of Venice, and strangely enough, no one noticed it. Was it because at that hour the Venetians were indulging in drink? Was it because in a city with so many pigeons, no one could say there was one more?

When they arrived at twilight in front of the great palace of the Witches of the Grand Canal, the Wind was trembling with fear. "Ch-child," he stammered, "now tell me how we get in."

The little boy crawled out of the pigeon and turned the handle of the palace door. The door creaked open. The Witches, absent-minded, had forgotten to lock it!

It was the very evening of the Witches' Great Summer Ball. While the Witches were up in their bedrooms busily dressing, the little boy started the search of the palace's one hundred rooms. He began from the bottom. When the Wind pushed the pigeon into the wine cellar, there, out of the darkness, strutted a dragon.

"Oh! Oh!" gasped the Wind. "He will eat us!"

"How handsome I am! Quite a beauty!" the dragon was saying as he admired himself in a mirror.

"Have you seen the little flower-plant girl?" asked the little boy from inside the pigeon.

"Only beautiful princesses are fine enough for me to eat." And moving on, he began again: "How handsome I am! Quite a beauty!"

The little boy turned the pigeon around, and the Wind pushed it back up and onto the grand staircase. Hurrying down was an enormous ogre carrying a basket full of candles.

"Have you seen the little flower-plant girl?" asked the little boy.

"I have no time to speak or to think!" grumbled the ogre, rushing away.

"No one has seen her . . ." the little boy muttered.

Darkness had fallen, and downstairs the ball was about to begin. Gondolas filled with guests were arriving at the palace door. When finally the King and the Queen of Venice appeared, covered with gold and precious stones, everyone exclaimed, "Such beauty! Such splendor!"

More than anything else in the world, the Witches of the Grand Canal loved dancing. That night, after a flourish of trumpets, they received their guests gayly singing:

> *"We, gracious Witches*
> *Of the Grand Canal*
> *Graciously say to you,*
> *Forget the gloom, come dancing*
> *And soon you will see*
> *How lovely, how thrilling*
> *The world will be."*

By the time they all began to dance, the little boy was climbing to the palace's third floor . . .

There the Witches had their bedrooms. After he looked under every bed and under piles of ball gowns left over from their parties and found nothing, the little boy climbed up the palace tower. There, at the top of the stairs, was a closed door. On the door was written WITCH MOTHER.

"Don't go inside! She sucks blood and spits poison!" wailed the Wind.

"But perhaps the little girl is kept prisoner in there, and the Witch Mother will eat her," replied the little boy.

With a sob, the Wind said, "Oh, poor little one," and blew the door wide open.

"Madam, have you seen the little flower-plant girl?" asked the little boy.

"Don't bother me while I fly through the sky of Venice!" shrieked the Witch Mother.

"They are all mad in this house," said the Wind, trembling from head to foot. "Let's go back to the garden."

"I don't like the garden. I want to play with the little flower-plant girl," said the little boy, and sadly he started down to the ground floor. He had searched ninety-nine rooms—ninety-nine rooms and not one less—and had not found the slightest trace of the little flower-plant girl.

Only the ballroom was left to be searched. But how could she possibly be hidden in a room filled with all those dancing people?

When the pigeon appeared at the ballroom entrance, everyone was struck dumb by the sight.

"Mother is at it again. She has put herself inside that pigeon and come down to spoil our fun. Ignore her," the Witches whispered to each other.

As for the King, Queen, and courtiers, they said haughtily, "These silly Witches are trying to impress us with a homemade wooden pigeon. It should at least have been made of gold."

To show how displeased they were, they too ignored the pigeon and all went back to their dancing with even more abandon than before.

The little boy began his inspection of the ballroom. He looked here and he looked there. He looked under chairs and under tables. Finally the pigeon had rolled over too many people's feet.

"Away, pigeon!" they all cried. "Away!" And they shoved the pigeon into a dark corner.

"Let's go back to the garden," repeated the Wind, but the little boy didn't answer.

"The little girl is lost forever . . ." he murmured, "and I will never play wonderful games with her. Now I am the only little flower-plant child in the world."

The dancers were whirling about the room at the peak of their gaiety, but inside the pigeon the little boy was crying.

But all of a sudden . . .

The crystal pendants of the chandelier began to tinkle. Then they tinkled louder. The sound was almost music.

How marvelous! Among those glittering pendants the little boy saw a tiny hand, and the tiny hand was jingling the pendants to signal him.

It was the little flower-plant girl! She was in the chandelier! The Witches had thought, "People don't hide little girls inside chandeliers, so let us put her up there."

"Who are you?" whispered the little girl.

"I've come to free you!" whispered the little boy.

"Oh, thank you!" she said.

The little boy told the Wind, "Blow, blow!" The Wind blew with all his breath. And while the King, Queen, Witches, and courtiers all went tumbling down with their feet high in the air, the little flower-plant girl jumped into the pigeon.

Just then dawn broke. The Sun jubilantly appeared and made the dry branches of the pigeon burst into leaf.

The pigeon stretched his leafy green wings and flew away through the window.

"Oh, dear, has something happened?" asked the Witches and the courtiers, trying to get back on their feet. But no one knew, because that night they all had danced too much and far too long.

Only the King of Venice saw everything, and he said, "I saw nothing."

The pigeon carried the little girl and the little boy high into the glorious sky of Venice, soaring and diving and circling—and their good friends the Sun and the Wind were with them. And this was indeed one of the wonderful games that only little flower-plant children can play.